Drums In Our Veins

Drums In Our Veins

Karen Georgia A. Thompson

Illustrated by Lynnette Li

———

Pink Owl Publishing LLC

Drums In Our Veins

Published by Pink Owl Publishing LLC

Library of Congress Control Number: 2021951586

ISBN (paperback): 9781662915901
eISBN: 9781662915918

tribute

To my parents Amybelle and Isaiah Thompson
who encouraged me to walk to the beat of my own drum.
May their voices be heard in the beat of the drums
as they journey with the Ancestors.

the rhythmic flow

Kenya: bongo

drum roll

"The drum is the favorite instrument of the spirits."
—African Proverb

Africa and Me

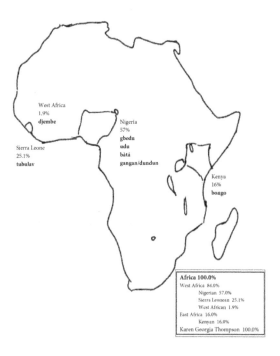

West Africa
1.9%
djembe

Nigeria
57%
gbedu
udu
bàtá
gangan/dundun

Sierra Leone
25.1%
tubulav

Kenya
16%
bongo

Africa 100.0%
West Africa 84.0%
Nigerian 57.0%
Sierra Leonean 25.1%
West African 1.9%
East Africa 16.0%
Kenyan 16.0%
Karen Georgia Thompson 100.0%

Africa 100

he said: it's not possible
I said: it is true

test came back
they read my DNA
said Africa 100
Africa in me
I knew

he said: DNA test is not science
I said: doesn't need to be

what does science have to do
with what the soul knows
Africa—west and east
Africa—shore to shore
Africa is in me

he said: nobody is 100%
I asked: is that a fact?

since this woman is not "nobody"
I claim that 100% as my truth
the DNA test was not free
it brought me back to this Africa
Africa is me

I said: Africa 100 is simplest of math
he said: your math does not add up

West 84 plus east 16
spell it out if you must
Nigeria, Sierra Leone, Kenya
and an identified bit of the west
Africa 100 percent present affirmed by DNA test

13 November 2020
12:30
Olmsted Township, OH
KGAT

meet the drums

The drums of Africa called me, in ways none
could explain, a rhythm and beat poured into my
soul, a beat calling me home. What my birth
certificate did not reflect, my soul knew beyond
words. Each day as I sat and listened to the beat of
the drums, words unspoken kept calling me back
to a home I had never known.

I took a DNA test because I wanted to know
where I came from, beyond the shores of the
island of Jamaica where I was born. I wanted to
know where my people came from, from which
land they were bought and sold. The test came
back and provided confirmation of truths
affirming my place in the world as a child of
traditions and people who knew the land, knew
God and understood the Universe in ways no one
taught me. The traditions and ways were coursing
through my DNA, they were always with me,
there was Knowing and Gift in my blood.

I chose these drums because they represent some of the drums of Africa, the land from which my Ancestors came. Each drum a part of the land and people coursing through my veins. I am who I am because they came to these shores, the beat of their drums lives in my veins.

The Ancestors are present with me for this journey, wherever it may lead.

Nigeria: Gbedu

Prelude

the beat

"When I was growing up,
they said there were people who could hear
the voices of the Ancestors
in the beat of the drums.
Maybe you are one of those people..."

Amybelle Adassa Thompson
Brooklyn, New York
May 2017

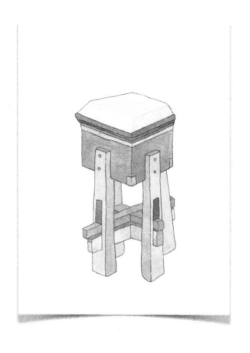

Sierra Leone/Jamaica: gumbeh

defiant drummers

Drum sound rises on the air, its throb, my heart.
A voice inside the beat says, "I know you're tired,
but come. This is the way."
—*Rumi*

my story

this child of kings and queens
this queen, matriarch
this king, leader

carrying stories in buckets
waters from deep wells
drawn daily

to quench my thirst
for free

a foretaste of glory
I will see

this is my story
this is my song

I am a laborer
in the fields
working the land

hands numb
fingers calloused
back bent to the sun

no time to weep
children cannot eat tears

this?
this is my land?

this is my story
this is my song

I am a laborer
in the fields
wearing stripes

moving rocks and stones
breaking up fallow ground
chains to my ankles

head bowed low
escaping the whip

punished for aspiring
punished for daring to own
myself as human

this is my story
this is my song

I am a laborer
in the fields
body sold to toil and till

no longer free
told I am worth
less than a horse

more than a mule
talking beast

beaten for thinking
shamed for being
fighting for purchase on my humanity

this is my story
this is my song

yesterday
was 577 years

today
577 years later

I sing the same story
I sing the same song

wailing for freedom
singing for change

broken bodies
broken promises

577 years of grave injustices
blessed assurance
justice will be mine

this is my story
this is my song

I am a laborer
in the fields
I toil in the heat

sweat on my brow
I smile at the sun
watching the children play
bringing water to pale visitors

I sing
murmuring the discordant beginning
of 577 years

this is my story
this is my song

4 April 2018
00:58
Washington, DC
KGAT

voices of the seas

listen to the voices
traveling on the waves
telling their stories of resistance

whispers heard in the spray.

millions of voices
silenced in the deep
tales amassed over years

tears felt in the spray.

stories of distress
theft and abuse
ships overloaded

cargo thrown to the spray.

generations buried
bones turned sand
humanity deprived

rights drowned in the spray.

water overwhelming
no announcements in the news
lives overtaken

bodies covered in the spray.

hear the whispers rising
voices getting louder
drowned in shallow waters

silence echoed in the spray.

people under water
unable to float
voiceless, unidentified

whispers heard in the spray.

7 May 2018
14:38
Willemstad, Curaçao
KGAT

barely breathing

crossings and musings
souls stirring
swimming sounds
of drums
drowning
this pain
redeeming their souls
telling our truth
here is breathing

I want to write history
I have stories to tell
stories
with no gilded edges
with no ending planned
stories of shame
stories of death
stories of wrongs ignored
stories of life beyond the sea
here is breathing

memories of trees
manifesting the Divine
in their leaves
met with violence
axe to trunk
transporting people
stacked as logs
there leaves
another ship
blessed by their God
cursing our souls
who are we?

these are not fairy tales
yet they tell of
Once upon a time
in a faraway land
full of sunshine
when royalty
was Black
Kings and Queens
building wealth without castles
loving our black skin
kissed by the sun
set gems
like moon light
leaning on the water
here is breathing

walking in power
at one with the earth
reading time
in the dust
hearing rain
in the silence
the future carried on the wind
the voice of the Mystery
heard in the drums
drunk on wisdom sublime
here is breathing

no superficiality to express
to will myself to experience you
Black faces
Black voices
God is black
seen in me
created in Divine image
Black as me
I am no orphan
a child of these Kings and Queens
sold by a depraved theology
brought to a wilderness
no drums
appeasing this torture
here is breathing

beyond the sea
at home among the dead

named as animal
trotting out
at the whim of the other
trotting in
to their deprived communities
whips
absent of love
bruises
absent of grace
rape
absent of this God
they said was so great
what then of me?
stay in suffocation?
no air to breathe

whey di card ah go draw
for a church built on lies
friends of all
neutral in silence
promoting the supremacy of one
praising a God white
missionaries stepping up
affirming the conditions
of the enslaved
sanctioning land grabs
exploiting Black lives
robbing Black identity
no breath in this Body

whey di card ah go draw
for a church built on Empire
missing social capital
sipping sugared coffee and tea
selling pie in the sky
to transported Ancestors
grabbing at gold
grasping at glory
grappling with God
a corrupt cocktail
of a hierarchal system
drunk on power
bloated with greed
beaten with the Bible
to ensure obedience
strangling our souls
where is the Life?

beyond the sea
there is me
Black skin
shining in the sun
sanity questioned
because I dare to question
being locked up
locked in
to the madness of inequity
remembering the crack of the whip
yet defying slave drivers
standing up strong in my identity

keeping myself in the knowledge
of the warriors from whom I came
here is breathing

beyond the sea
resisting the will to be complicit
to the diminishment of light
of breath in bodies
in a system where class, caste, color
are used to concoct
separate yet equal
low wages for some
mass incarceration
unemployment
poverty
if we stay in sufferation
swallowing the bile
of trauma
fueled by those who taught
the skin I am in
is sin
nothing right
words strangling my life
if we not part of the change
then we part a di degradation
here is breathing

learning from it all
I am royalty
I am a supreme expression of the Divine

I am history that did not begin or end with
enslavement
I am the wind in the trees, the voice on the breeze
I am the wisdom of the Ancestors
I am rich with melanin
I am all hues and shades of brown
another legacy of Ancestors transported
I am breathing

21 February 2018
00:15
Kingston, Jamaica
Karen Georgia A. Thompson
Keon Heywood

no apology

explorers
laying claim to what was not lost
riding at will the high seas

encountering lands
people labeled as strange
disbursing deliberate deceit

on the journeys
they were praying and singing
claiming Jesus the only way

center is where you project you sit
supremacy your true god
off center the hold on majority rights
possessing pilfered properties

colonizing minds
bullying your way
bringing terror to humanity

history repeated

for hundreds of years
burying bullied bodies

rehearsing contrived speeches
manufacturing hate
claiming Jesus the only way

pushing and shoving unrepentantly
weeping to have your own way
no excuses untapped
coopting cultures, crushing civilizations

sociology, anthropology
concocted race theories
building controlling theologies

what of this Jesus?
identify your gods
capitalism, colonialism, church

6 March 2018
14:15
Arusha, Tanzania
KGAT

my Ancestors

your memories
echo
through the silence
hundreds of years
your quantified pain
ignored
for financial gain.

your bones
line
the floor of the Atlantic
your blood
painting
walls of castles
long empty.

the Ancestors weep
their dreams kept alive
in those who do not sleep

your bodies
used

as whipping posts
machines to till and plow
your life owned
treated like animals
bought and sold.

your spirits
speak
from unmarked graves
where bodies planted
provide no rest for souls
fighting for life and right
even in death.

the Ancestors weep
their hopes kept alive
in those who do not sleep

your voices
live
stories emerging
as you persist
speaking truth from the beyond
telling tales of injustice
long erased

your children
listen
your whispers
in the drums

breathing words unheard
demanding justice
for your own

the Ancestors weep
their courage kept alive
in those who do not sleep

21 January 2016
14:00
Lakewood, OH
KGAT

UN-*sanitized*

(the un-sanitized version)

I tried to teach my sons what my parents
attempted to teach me
they tried to keep me safe
they did their best to warn me
there are rules, they said
rules to be upheld
these rules unwritten
these rules filled my head
these rules kept me in check
institutionally chained
these rules kept me sanitized with these rules
there was shaming and pain

keep your mouth shut
avert your eyes
hands on the wheel
no moves that surprise
no fancy cars
no fancy clothes

learn your place
keep your disdain off your face
I played by the rules
I taught my kids
be polite
to follow those rules

smile when you are pissed
keep your hands where they can be seen
bring your anger home
don't show your rage
in the streets
don't run after dark
dress the right way
don't walk in a pack
that guarantees
you stay off the front page

the more polite I am
the more that boot presses into my neck
my anger must be kept in check
gloriously sanitized
while your ill-will and hate
is fed like shit on a plate
the open hatred you display
the fearless way you name your disdain
I must swallow like a pill
as my words get stuffed in my throat again

to not be that angry Black bitch
I must keep my mouth shut
nod my head
shrink into your back room
well, here's the news
I was never one to cower
I will no longer de-sanitize myself
in the confines of my shower
in an attempt to keep you satisfied
when you are so damned wrong

the hot water cannot remove the staining
of your words
the soap cannot cleanse
the rage you provoke
I am choking to death every day
on the anger I swallow
every time I go out

go do your work
re-educate yourself
you are not better because you said
so, get your fucking boot
off my god-damned neck
I will no longer "watch my words"
I will no longer fear your stinking jails
I will no longer allow you to define me as unsafe
my un-sanitized self you will meet today

with your guns, your privilege, your pale
I afforded you grace
the scriptures you used said that was my place
I suggest you not confuse me with the Holy
or use my race as some deep disgrace
my anger you will meet
I will walk on able feet
rather than sit and swallow the shit you mete

so step back slowly out of my space
you will not determine my worth
you will not determine my words
you will not write my script
I will be heard
the fear is gone
the revolution has begun
remember
you heard it here first

16 November 2015
Plane—ATL to CLE
KGAT

the margins

living on the edge
this is no adventure
life undefined
risking all to live
suffering to exist
I am danger.

living on the edge
a perilous lifestyle
disregarded
unsheltered
nothing to own
pushed to the edge
no food to eat
I am labelled.

living on the edge
margins pushing in
living off the center
hiding from myself
hidden by the center

I no longer exist.

28 November 2017
10:20
Bangkok, Thailand
KGAT

seen

before the mirror
I stand

eyes staring back
looking for truth
examining beauty
I see God in me

before the world
I stand

waiting in line
watching as the other
steps in front of me
I am unseen

before the mirror
I stand

strength unqualified
spirit unchained
beauty uncharted

I am free

before the church
I stand

heard as articulate
seen as a number
touched without notice
I am invisible

before the mirror
I return

eyes filled with tears
looking for beauty
examining my truth
I see God in me

before the world
I stand

broken, bruised, wounded
by word
by attitudes
rendered afraid
because I am

before the church
I stand

overlooked by dismissive eyes
unseeing my Black self
unseen by Whiteness
damning me to a hell
rendered invisible
by hatred

I see me
I am enough
I am the Universe

2 October 2017
15:47
Edmonton, AB
KGAT

fast

running, screaming
pain on the streets
the silence echoes
why now?
why me?

running hard
running fast
from poverty
from despair
the silence of my footsteps
none choose to hear

running to freedom
running for fresh air
running for clean water
does anyone care?

running as fast as I can
running for my life
from stray bullets in the hood
from the guns of the man

running to the light
running from the theft of my soul
running because there is none
to save memories
running
hungry to be free

I am running
running every day
running
going fast to nowhere

5 October 2017
22:00
Seattle, WA
KGAT

masks

I am centered
I am unafraid
lost and alone
in the crowd
my mask in place
a smile on my face

I am well
I am healed
this you will see
my wounded heart
my broken spirit
buried deep beneath
a smile on my face

I am educated
I am promise
moving gracefully
no home to decorate
no food to eat
my troubles overwhelm
a smile on my face

I am wonderful
I am lovely
my anger bubbles
my rage seethes
my control erupts
a smile on my face

I am brokenhearted
I am unwell
devastated
losing hope
darkness consumes
the weight of life
pulls me under
I sink
a smile on my face

29 November 2017
9:46
Bangkok, Thailand
KGAT

Whispers in the Sugar Cane Fields

(from the Pacific to the Atlantic)

the smell of rain in the air
the clean crisp earth
stained with blood
bodies in chains
the smell rising across the soil
assaults the senses
unmasking the sharp edges
of the leaves
moving gently
whispering softly
in the sugar cane fields

blue sunshine filled skies
a promise of the future
distant
instead in the hush of the morning
clouds roll across the skies
rain lightly falling
no sound
the silence of death
in the sugar cane fields

where did time go?
not the night or the morning
years flying swiftly on vast wings

while I was sleeping
growing sunspots and wrinkles
generations dead
worked like machines
treated like animals
in the sugar cane fields

this sky
this rain
prophecy
of the storm to come
waters to cleanse
to sweep away the injustice and the unjust
thunder to bellow the rage and the fear
of exploited labor
named slaves
in the sugar cane fields

this storm
not first or last
change is inevitable
like the growth of the stalk
planted with hatred
watered with pain
consuming lives
the muck of the soil
corruption and greed
rebellion rises
fueled by need
another generation beaten
in the sugar cane fields

the stalks whisper
telling tales of yesterday and tomorrow
telling of sorrow
recalling horrors
of sweet powder extracted
while robbing the sweetness
of dignity and freedom
leaving behind broken bodies
with the bitterness of molasses
yesterday is today
in the sugar cane fields

the skies open up
refusing to hold on to secrets
of generations in the sun
bruised and beaten
letting go of all these skies have seen
the screams gone unheard
no longer silent
the lightning flashes
the thunder roars
rejecting silence
weeping loudly
mourning the losses
in the sugar cane fields

3 December 2017
14:53
Washington, DC
KGAT

Nigeria: gangan/dundun
(talking drum)

compelling call

Misery don't call ahead. That's why you
have to stay awake—otherwise it just
walks on in your door.
—Toni Morrison

out of my head

the silence haunts me
the memories long dead
the pain forgotten,
resurrected
lingering,
casting shadows across my heart
rushing waters of despair overtake me
pulling me under

why this wrestling
with the self
this quest for sense amidst
the nonsense of times gone by
of ills and wounding that refuse
to remain buried
in the graveyard of the soul

there are no tears
to quench the dryness of these bones
scattered, without care
skeletal remains of dreams
the decaying carcasses of hopes
buried alive

morose grows wild
like untreated ivy up the walls
of my heart
threatening to strangle
to rid my body of breath
of desires that lurk in visions
of happiness
in thoughts of love
in schemes of being me

the silence
a mirror reflecting
that which stares into it
revealing truths
screaming to be heard
truths that are the din
which scare and open
refusing to go quietly
unwilling to hide

this fight,
warring with the self
attempting to surface the authentic
to lay bare the places that are moss laden
the places where light now shines brightly
the light of silence
that illuminates fears, disguised as past hopes
the light that reveals
pain is not forgotten

the darkness is a fallacy
the wounds
the bruises
the tears
are no longer hidden in the silence
itself a door swung open
a door that invites
letting go of the shame that is darkness

why struggle
rest in the silence
embrace the beauty of stillness
nurturing new life
close the eyes to the known
let the Spirit be guide
reach up and out
of head into the knowing of the heart

15 March 2017
22:40
Lakewood, OH
KGAT

Black Lives

our stories untold
our stories erased from history books
slave ships in abundance
the voices of the Ancestors do not lie
their cries come on the waves of the Atlantic
their screams come on the swirl of trade winds.

our uniqueness is our diversity
bodies left as cargo in every port
our millions every religion, every hue
what of the stories of the shame and the pain?
who tells our stories?
who hears our pain?

stories of robbers who stole our children
they stole our men and women too
stories of the great lie, of the great deception
they brewed
while sipping tea in Timbuktu
plucking diamonds from our minds
they told us we sold each other
that was their lie.

they told us we were no good
we were one hundred pounds worth
a one-time purchase for their fields
a machine for their work
they told us our bodies were an atrocity
as they raped us with penis and eyes
they lied when they took us
leaving our families behind
no letters, no rescue, false hopes.

they lied in the Middle Passage
they lied yet again
they promised forty acres
and one mule
lying as they went.

who will tell the stories
of their infidelity, selling our daughters
breeding our men
the cruelty of the whip
we were named as animals
they lied
these Christians
who brought their guns with their Bibles.
they lied about the Mystery
said we did not know
what we saw in the trees
what we heard in the leaves
we saw in the hills
we respected in the plains

on the clouds, and in the sunrise
we knew there was no unknowing
The One beyond names.

they lied about our children
told us we could not read
our inventions they took as their own
we found our way to schools
imparted wisdom to each other
rescue came
Maroons fled on foot to the hills
others the Underground Railroad
the rebellions and uprisings
what did they expect?
the rivers and lakes joined our protests

these lives have their stories to tell
the Ancestors call from unmarked graves
through the jungles of distant continents
from the depths of rivers
from the caverns of oceans
from the bellies of dogs
fed with their bones
the Ancestors weep.

who will tell the stories of the lands
where we landed
of the companies we built
of the railroads we laid
of the Panama Canal we dug.

who will tell the stories
of our brilliance shining bright
from the places where we were buried
of our resurrection
from beds where we died every night
from the grief of our children taken
from the stripes wailed on our backs
of our collective miseducation
unemployment, underemployment
of the modern day slavery that is
minimum wage, trafficking
our children killing each other
for scraps left on the floor.

who will tell the story
of our unity we are one
dispelling myths that feed us lies
that we don't love
can't love
won't love
each other.

matters not where we come from
continent or diaspora
here is the news
we were all bought and sold
we were all commodified
we were all used
we were all sold the same lie

24 October 2015
8:35
Phoenix, AZ
KGAT

blooming bones

*The hand of the Lord came upon me, and he
brought me out by the spirit of the Lord and
set me down in the middle of a valley; it was
full of bones. He led me all around them;
there were very many lying in the valley, and
they were very dry. He said to me, "Mortal,
can these bones live?" (Ezekiel 37:1-3)*

valley of dry bones
absent of life
Can these dry bones live?
evidence of wanting
a stockpile of life gone
piled high to the sky
devoid of breath
no purpose
none collecting
none commenting
all watching
these dry bones
none to prophesy

standing in the valley
staring at these bones
their confounded presence
haunting the living
their brittle dryness
glistening in the sun
filtering through leaves
their stark whiteness
contrasting grass
green of trees
fertile earth brown
bodies
no longer flesh and breath
Can these dry bones live?
who will prophesy?

what died
leaving this valley of bones?
the breath
of our humanity?
our will to live love?
disparaging skin
as sin
decrying gender
as inferior
depicting human sexuality
as ungodly
prophesy to the dryness
bringing breath to the slain

who died
leaving this valley of bones?
is this pile of whiteness
African Ancestors long passed?
our black and brown children
prematurely taken
mistaken as threat?
their white bones
in the sun
mocking the glorification of whiteness
undistinguishable
from the bones of bitter oppressors
who will prophesy to these bones?

standing in the valley
staring at these bones
listening to the breadth
of a past forgotten
wishing for the wisdom
of Ancestors crying
bones weeping dryness
tears unseen
as the clouds roll over
the sky opens
speaking into this valley
waters rolling down
bringing a new thing
blowing from the four winds

tear drops
rain drops
waters of hope
splashing dreams and visions
the Mystery
of dust turned mud
pollen from trees
these bones live
from them emerge petals
blooming bones
in the valley
a new generation
watching hope emerge
standing in the valley
staring at these bones
prophesying truth

26 March 2018
7:56
Macdonough, GA
KGAT

we talk

I am
she begins
then the confusion
brows furrow
she travels
to the other side
silence descends
I wait
she returns

you came knowing
she says
knowing everything
the wisdom of the world
in your eyes
the vision of Creator
emitting from your being
fingers fisting purpose
the Ancestors present
naming you Gift
and gifted

I am
she continues
the child of my parents
and their parents
them African
named as slaves
they no slaves
enslaved
she closes her eyes

you came knowing
healing with your presence
open to the world
hearing God
listening to the Ancestors
living in a world
defined by knowing
seeing the unseen
calling out
breathing the unnamed
you can See, she said

30 December 2017
Brooklyn, NY
KGAT

interrupted

fire in my belly
tears streaming down my face
listening to the interpretations
of love, unity and grace
emitting from hearts of stone
no compassion present
another day of brutality
with people who lost their way

the fires burn
infernos rage
fueled by despondency
burning down our lives
leaving ashes mixed with tears
this living with people who lost their way

all are equal is optional
"*imago dei*" is rhetoric
singing songs of healing
with lyrics creating wreckage
naming sin as gospel
absent of effective witness

love enacted selectively
selling hope alongside misery

the fires burn
infernos rage
fueled by despondency
burning down our lives
leaving ashes mixed with tears
ignored by people who lost their way

refusing to see all are not free
while refuting the Doctrine of Discovery
in the face of differences
what of the quest for transformation?
in the face of racism
where is this love they continue to mention?
another day of hopelessness
where is this faith of possibility?
when living with people who lost their way

the fires burn
infernos rage
fueled by despondency
burning down our lives
leaving ashes mixed with tears
iniquitous people who lost their way

I witness again liberal betrayal
progressive self-interest
on display

clothed in demands for justice
these people who lost their way
decrying hunger
disregarding lives
another day of brutality
with people who lost their way

8 March 2018
11:34
Arusha, Tanzania
KGAT

the risk of being

what is the story
you want me to tell you?

healing the individual
wounding social contexts
transformation
politicization
change the system
preferential option for the poor

what is the story
you want to hear?

2 October 2017
Brooklyn, NY
KGAT

a place to call home

my heart longs for home
to feel the roots of life
extending from my toes

for that place
where my soul connects
to my Ancestors long gone

I long for home

30 January 2010
23:26
Lakewood, OH
KGAT

Going Home

the waves hit the shores
their thunder crying out my name

their waters welcoming me home
inviting me
telling me what I longed to know
bellowing an abiding love for me

amidst my own longing
for these shores, for these seas

the beauty of home
seen from great heights

the greens of the mountains
the blues of the seas
the sun in the sky

the wind whispering
the trees swaying
to pulsing island rhythms
echoing my heartbeat

the air is the very blood
coursing through my veins

this land of my birth
refusing to let me go
these Ancestors of mine
refusing to let me go

across time and space
they call me
beckoning me
"Come my child!"

calling me into knowing and rest
renewal and deep longing

to sit under the trees
and listen

to stand
on the shores and see

who I am

to recognize the woman
I am called to be

these roads are my journey
to myself
revealing more

than I imagined
I am or could be

Home called me
going Home
changed Me

2 January 2016
9:29
Lakewood, OH
KGAT

no hands for time

trapped
longing for a past
glorified by colossal husks
topped with mammoth gilded steeples
turned behemoth albatross
standing in ravaged lots
no one stopping or curious
no major loss
feeding greedily
on borrowed time

confused
discussing definitions
with language promoting servile submission
exclusively naming selective inclusivity
amidst an absence
of diverse races
condemning dark faces
navel gazing
drinking wine
on borrowed time

broken
seeking relevance
while damming waters to dry places
stopping spirits destined to join
the Ocean wide
busy counting empty spaces
no opinions worth naming
dreaming of excess
planting graves
on borrowed time

fixated
fixing itself
no hands to lend
refusing to help
watching countless young lives waste away
endowments and planned giving
mounting crosses on dilapidated buildings
deliberating a fading history
on borrowed time

disenchanted
preaching poverty
light of the world
rehearsing philosophies
missing purpose and rudderless
with no rewind
a broken clock
with no tick tock
who needs hands

when you long stopped
wasted away yesterday
on borrowed time

11 October 2017
14:17
Cluj Napoca, Romania
KGAT

step back

miles away from home
in places you chose to ignore
you nurse your guilt
sipping whiteness
through gilded straws
your eyes opening
to what you selectively feel free to see

expect no sympathy
no empathy from me
why not in your home?
what? not in your back yard?
tell my why your concern is now

miles away from home
your guilt washes
over you as you hear
unemployment is high
families are displaced
racism is rampant
inequalities abound

your tears are bitter
a watershed that does not move me
your disdain
now coupled
with this guilt you haul around

dry your tears
resist the need to theorize
miss me
with your gentrified lies
I have no pity
for your first world revelations
your response is no surprise

check your history
talk to your ancestors
let them help you
to new knowledge
decolonize

you live in a country built on lies
a country with a history
you choose to sterilize
whitening the darkness of enslavement
slave ships turned immigrant vessels
the rape of our Mothers
now the enticement of white men

your ancestors pillaged and sold
you do much the same

your tears are your shame
the flood much too late
your feigned generosity and charity
misplaced
with your "new found" awakening

September 2017
6:01
Somewhere in Europe
KGAT

West Africa: djembe/jembe

healing tones

Take a day to heal from the lies you've told yourself
and the ones that have been told to you.
—Maya Angelou

beyond time

drums
beating loud and strong
speaking across time
traveling across space
my heart echoing the beat
giving rhythm to the blood
connecting generations
coursing through my veins

drums
beating loud and strong
giving voice to the pain
of the Ancestors long gone
whispering joy to a people
determined to be witnesses
to the magnitude of the created

drums
beating loud and strong
signaling change
giving beat to resistant feet
running to be free
beating out the sounds of longing
offering courage in a depraved wasteland

drums
beating loud and strong
hearing beyond the sound
heralding the faith that springs eternal
giving rise to the strength
to overcome
chains on my mind
tying my spirit down

drums
beating loud and strong
the wisdom of Ancestors
visioning the impossible
calling liberation to the mind
healing for the body
pounding out words of self-worth
giving beat to the wings of freedom

drums
beating loud and strong
bringing hope to desolate places
naming wrongs in the breath of a song
brothers and sisters hearing promises
mothers and fathers stitching a future
carried on the beat that is
beyond time

3 December 2017
13:30
Washington, DC
KGAT

flying at dusk

into the darkness
while others rest
when life slows
at the end of the day
you wait patiently
for sun to set
for leaves to quiet their sway
alert, eyes open
you wait.

into the darkness
where fears abound
where anxieties increase with speed
you find your best self
alone in your quest
welcoming the silence
on which you glide.

into the darkness
where night consumes day
where stars are seen
and moon shines bright

a place misunderstood
its beauty missed by most
where others shroud
their malice, their lies,
their vicious intent.

into the darkness
you find your own mystery
borne on wings spread wide
eyes that see all
intuition beyond hearing
you fly into its freedom
until the morning.

1 November 2015
7:07
Lakewood, OH
KGAT

unscripted

there is that day
one amazing day
where time unwinds
in stationary restlessness
beckoning

the hours unfurl uninterrupted
soft
like moon kissed petals
covered with dew
under the early morning sun

each minute we are transformed
moments taken in stride
finding
laughter amidst strangeness
joy in the mundane

like waters meandering
wistfully
through flowered concrete canals
making our way through busy streets

we journey

invited unknowingly
to drink from deep wells
walking the unfamiliar
repeatedly
we tread uncharted pathways

seeking salves for sapped souls
looking
for the obvious to mend fragmented lives
we encounter magic
in letting go

our unnoticed emptiness
is replenished
gazing at the sacred beauty of existing
today
where life finds us

walking in the sun
we find
ourselves
unscripted partners
writing memories with Mystery

finding what we did not seek
we rediscover the timelessness of self
renewed
we rid ourselves
of brokenness

remembering
we are healed
all we need we find
standing in the stillness
today

in the end
our hearts replete with wonder
we watch the world go by
from neon lighted street corners
grateful

15 May 2018
6:49
Seoul, South Korea
KGAT

life cycles

in the midst of a sunny day
the clouds came
sun on the left
a reminder of better times
sun on the right
a witness of times to come

in the moment
the skies darkened
the clouds lowered
then the rains
beating into the ground
new life comes

why run from the present
why ignore the beauty
the cycles of life
harnessed in one raindrop
holding in its essence
yesterday, today
heralding tomorrow

watch and see the darkness roll in
be at one with yourself
pain a reminder of humanity
grief a reminder of cycles
this present
a call
beckoning
move on

4 August 2018
15:49
Fort Lauderdale Beach, FL
KGAT

rainbows in the rain

gloom descends ahead of the storm
blue skies give way to clouds

grey dominates
shrinking the horizon

beauty flutters by on reluctant leaves
pulled by winds unseen

the restless soul meanders these shores
pushed by unseen anguish

uncertainty descends ahead of the rain
stirring fears long buried

whipping doubt into a frenzy
darkness creeps in billowing in the silence

destinations become irrelevant
in this present where stillness ensues

in the loud hush of wind passing by
possibilities appear in the distance

glimmers of light
breaking through as yellow slicing grey

blue descends once again
opening a new path through impossibility

welcoming into this moment
wisdom arriving on swift wings

revelation a dense shower
washes away the decay and empowers

what then of this dreary state of unrest?
as light breaks forth arresting the din

where the mind gives way to new hope within
we wait for the colors to change

watching life give birth to new realities
rainbows falling in raindrops

1 June 2018
20:14
Chicago, IL
KGAT

painting pictures

let fly the words you hear
tumbling
like sacred waters falling
let fly the words that come
silent
on the wings of owls
flying into the dusk
to sleep with the morning

let fly the words you hear
vibrant
like paint on butterfly wings
let fly the words that come
painting
the joy of your heart
echoing
the wounds deep within

let fly the words you hear
visiting
in the drops on a rainy day
let fly the words that come
drifting
like clouds taking shape
on a sunny day

let fly the words you hear
spinning
your tales like spider webs
let fly the words that come
bless the words that leave
floating
away on a summer breeze

let fly these words you hear
feel the life they bring
stories that enter from without
stories poured from within
let fly the words that come
on the first breath of morning light
singing new life
planting new hope
with the unfolding sun rise

let them fly
these words
they cannot die
adrift across time and space
let fly these words
a gift of beauty to share
let them go
painting pictures on their way

8 October 2017
20:54
Cluj-Napoca, Romania
KGAT

complicit

measure the silence
in beats of compassion
how long before you speak
the world needs your voice
to speak while others weep
silence is for those who sleep.

measure the silence
in the breaths between their screams
how long before you hear
the sounds of hearts breaking
in defeat and despair
silence is for those who don't care.

measure the silence
in the depths of their teardrops
another child dies
in her mother's arms
hunger gnaws at their bellies
no food for miles
silence is for those spewing bile.

measure the silence
in the heartbeats of the hopeless
cry because you must
because your soul aches for justice
grasping at peace
no need for despair
silence is for those who won't hear.

measure the silence
in the syllables of repackaged truth
the system is abusive
justice is elusive
scream your truth
run from hate and fear
silence is for those who are living dead.

7 December 2017
18:18
Honolulu, HI
KGAT

uninhibited

on the beach
clouds rolling by
telling their stories
ancient blessings sung
as time marches on
you wait

sitting in the sands
listening to the waves
grains sticking to wet skin
waters rolling in tandem rhythm
unfettered beauty on display
you wait

the sounds of the ocean
bringing the voices of Ancestors
long gone
the silence of the clouds
writing memories of Ancestors
long forgotten
you wait

life finds you
as the crowds run away from the waters
seeking shelter
from the wetness of rain
as the skies open up
the waters pour
you find yourself

yours is the center
your life the beauty of the Universe
your existence transformed
by a magnificent journey
wrought on untamed waters
carrying you
beyond the seas

you stay and watch the waters roll in
you realize the gift of these rains
the gift of this storm
the gods unnamed
revealing themselves
a reminder
you are not alone

the burdens ease
the weight shifts
the water pellets sting your skin
rain drops beat the waters
rain drops beat the sand

rain drops beat the memories away
leaving you whole

each moment leaves you uninhibited
you dance in the waters of the sky
you welcome a healing promised
you let go of centuries of wonder
realizing that all that is unnamed
all that is mystery
is all that you are named to be

4 August 2018
15:29
Fort Lauderdale Beach, FL
KGAT

mother to daughter

For Julia and Sara

your tear stained face visits
my sick bed
your eyes grow wide
searching mine for signs of life
your hands gently wipe
my sweat drenched body
your warm even breath
mingles with my gasps for air

you are the child I wished for
from womb to cradle
you are the child I knew
in my heart
the child I carried and cared for
the beauty I rocked to sleep
now
you do the same for me

in my wildest dreams
in my distant imaginings
in my daydreams good and bad
this picture of me

this picture of you
never materialized
my heart hurts
my strength leaves

my daughter
the little girl I know
I watched you grow
your pretty brown eyes
your joyous laughter
your fun filled curiosity
blossoming, blooming
into a beautiful sun kissed flower

at twenty
your responsibilities outweigh my own
school, home, two jobs
yet you come to care for me
your days running thirty-six hours
your weeks eight days
the darkness under your eyes
tell me you lack sleep

my daughter
I am glad you found love
a greater love than I ever knew
you surpassed the models
you saw in my life
it's your time
I love you

spread your wings

say your goodbye
fly my daughter
fly

into the hope
your soul longs for
into the brightness
your great future holds
into the possibilities
your dreams will manifest
fly my daughter
fly

you will never forget
the direction of this nest
my heart longs
to know you are safe
my heart aches with the pain
you have now in this place
we will cry no more
fly

spread your wings my daughter
fly

18 March 2010
6:10
DTW-CLE
KGAT

grieving

I watched my Mommy die
over and over again she leaves
flying away from this world
a red bird high in the sky

her spirit rests with Ancestors
mine refuses to grieve
holding onto vibrant memories
longing for relief

perhaps I want her present
to reconsider
to make different choices
although she left at her scheduled time

the desire to hear her voice
does not ease my heartache
I eagerly await her return
anticipating a miraculous unnatural rebirth

my soul recognizes her essence
her wisdom visits in my dreams

her healing came at her letting go
my healing comes at letting her go

28 July 2018
17:22
Brooklyn, NY
KGAT

beyond basics

(For Giovan, Elijah, Sara)

the beauty of the world awaits
lofty mountains to see
with their distant peaks
covered in summer—white
waters rushing to places undiscovered
barreling over rocks unmoving
who unable or unwilling
slow not this hurried passing.

listen to their voices
find your way to embrace
their wisdom, their joy.

the wonder of being surrounds
a reminder that you are
tree, earth, sky, seed
filled with purpose
overflowing with a longing
for fingers to touch sky

like leaves on the tips of branches
reaching boldly into the unknown.

let them teach you of their dreams

their aspirations are yours
hear their whisper on a breeze.

the joy of life pulses
in the veins of leaves
that are the very food
nourishing the peoples who forgot
that they own nothing
not even breath loaned for time
short is the length of journey.

take nothing you didn't bring
respect all living
all your relations, of them sing.

the mystery of living
lies before you
a package of dreams, hopes
of longing that is your purpose
your part in the beauty, wonder, joy
open your heart
let your soul be fed
beyond the basics.
you will find
love already found you
hope that soars high on wings.

24 October 2015
7:20
Wyoming, MI
KGAT

Nigeria: bàtá

beats of resistance

True resistance begins with people confronting
pain...
and wanting to do something to change it.
—bell hooks

broken sidewalks

we, inhabitants of time and space
children of lesser gods
brothers and sisters of light
relatives
of saints and sinners

we, wounded travelers
building magical moving staircases
to fantastical dreams
traumatized healers
mending breaches and fissures

then as now
we rise
then as now
we hear the drumbeats of tomorrow

then as now
we chart a future
singing songs
without a score

then is now

we, the transcendent
children of the earth
babies formed from tears
visionaries writing
on the clouds

we, the mystery of life
living as seeds fallen into the cracks
of broken sidewalks
finding soil
pushing deep, shattering concrete

then as now
we flourish
then as now
we hold tight to each other

then as now
we chant incantations
weaving strength and hope
into broadcloth of justice

without looms

we, waters flowing free
children of breath
bearers of courage

luminaries of change
marching across broken sidewalks

we, creators of tranquility
children of radiant brilliance
defying obstacles
sidesteppers of defeat
building pathways to our destiny

then as now
we transmogrify
then as now
we swim rivers to generational healing

then as now
we dream afloat
riding flotsam
rearranging shards of broken sidewalks

into sweeping mosaics of freedom

3 April 2018
19:52
Washington, DC
KGAT

for generations

sing songs of freedom
celebrate your crowns
sing out without fear
dismiss the despair
celebrate!
you are kings and queens
yesterday
and today

sing strong
head held high
sing your songs
of freedom
live with hope
aspire to greatness
Great
is who you are

sing your dreams
into the night air
remember God close
as breath

manifested
in red, yellow, green, white
of Orishas, Lwas
called by many names

sing your joy
through the places
absent of light
stepping boldly
through muck and mire
celebrate you
fashioned in the brilliance
of the sun

sing as witnesses
to memories erased
your heart carrying the knowledge
of Ancestors long forgotten
into the light of morning
sing
beyond doubt
live into The Knowing
celebrate The Gift of you

19 February 2018
19:40
Kingston, Jamaica
KGAT

salvation (yours)

emptiness is not bliss
deep calls to deep
why temper in others what you seek
stifle what you cannot keep

14 October 2017
11:06
Paris, France
KGAT

salvation (mine)

running through the shallows
escaping soulless people
adrift on flotsam
hugging close to shore
wallowing in endless sorrow
wondering if tomorrow

clinging to ill-gotten visions
marketing souls
in heaps and storage bins
grabbing for power
living pretense
counting ruined lives
as wealth and strength

running through the shallows
heading for the deep
sidestepping broken dreams
unspoken hopes in the detritus
pulling
trying to slow me

myopic thoughts
closed doors
blocking my egress
from this wasteland
this wilderness
creating mass distress

running through the shallows
uncertainty ahead
no dread
embracing risk
leaving those soul stealers behind
to feed upon themselves

14 October 2017
10:45
Paris, France
KGAT

played out

call it a fiasco
call it one dirty disgrace
Open your eyes
Look! You will see
A sad truth, concocted
yesterday and today

This truth is conditional
A story of elaborate lies,
A story filled with erasures
A story rewritten to project and protect
That's no surprise

open the door
Gi wi the key
We will write our own history
our eyes are open
We will march.
We will shout.
We will not be locked out.

History cannot be owned
Is not for you to shelter an' key
No embarrassment this skin I am in
Race is not to display or entertain

Destinies charted in the temple of Black skin
The vestiges of history an ongoing sin
This temple is sacred and holy
Transcending the profane of the colonial unholy
Overcoming the arrogance of a self-privileged
race

open the door
Gimme di key
We will tell our own stories
our eyes are open
We will march.
We will shout.
We will not be locked out.

The voices of the Ancestors scream from the soil
Stories they have to tell
The stones spell out the wrongs you've done
The sunlight shines revealing all you attempt to
make dead

Claiming what you cannot own
Buying what is not for sale
Selling what you do not own
Building upon lives you easily displace

Laying waste to resources and land
Annihilating those who do not surrender and
stand
To the whiteness you wear and wield
Masquerading as legal tender
Clothed in brutality

open the damned door
We taking those keys
How dare you lock us out
Block our ears from our own story?

4 October 2017
14:11
Edmonton, AB
KGAT

missing pieces

calling me out of my name
staring at me with rage
rendering me out of place
looking
for your identity
claiming superior race

there is joy in knowing
who I am
where I come from
my Black skin you mock
resenting what I know
buying
time on orange beds
paying for more brown

naming yourself privileged
grazing lands far and wide
chasing your identity
stealing culture
Vultures
preying on humankind

there is peace in knowing
who you are
where you come from

mistaking
white for self-esteem
violence
for self-knowing

you raided the sacred places
tore down the altars we built
told me your god was better than mine
traded me your religion for my spirituality
repackaged and sold back to me over time

there is love in knowing
who you are
where you come from
heritage
you try to steal
like gold and diamonds and minerals
for these you sold your soul
threw away your identity

unfinished puzzles
a picture incomplete
picking pieces
trying to recreate
parts of me I will not hide
validating your white face

12 October 2017
20:25
Cluj Napoca, Romania
KGAT

playing with fire

fire of terror
fire by night
hatred on sticks
O, say can you see?
burning out your plight
burning down our homes
hooded masks you proudly wear
waving fear to control

fire on crosses
fire by night
casting shadows on oak leaves
witnessing temples swinging
by the dawn's early light
from these ancient trees
bringing torture and death
to what you tried to own
fire in your hand
flame missing from your soul
Black lives cannot be bought or sold

fire of spirit
fire by night
ours is no forgotten dream
fire in our hearts
fire in our bellies
lift every voice and sing
at the twilight's last gleaming

fire on lawns
fire by night
the neighborhood watch rides again
afraid of unarmed men and women
showing disregard for breathing children
good for your cotton fields
good for cleaning your floors
chasing lives on your terror rides
throwing cocktails at innocent doors
bombs bursting in air
the flag still flies

fire on streets
fire by night
bringing fresh terror to churches and Black lives
misplaced blame
still the source of your pain
wearing polo shirts and designer ties
whiteness the only hood you now wear
bringing your granddaddies' fire games
attempting evictions by fire and terror
tiki torches burning citronella

fire of spirit
fire by night
O'er the land of the free and the home of the
brave
fire in our hearts
fire in our bellies
marching and kneeling
at the twilight's last gleaming

10 October 2017
2:56
Cluj-Napoca, Romania
KGAT

shackled

Mary Mary quite contrary
worried about shackles on your feet
the chains you wear
invisible to see
walking unbound
you are not free

emancipate yourself from mental slavery
free yourself from your colonized mind
confused about values
a white god up above
no concept of who you are
no insight
no self-love

free your mind Miss Mary
you don't need to dance
miseducation is no cause for celebration
your mind in chains
wrapped up in self-hatred
and starched white aprons

Hey Mary Mary
how does your garden grow?

sing songs of freedom
not of broken chains you still carry
growing cotton in your mind
on plantations you designed
oppressed by concepts of god
whiteness unseen
voting for The Man
doing nothing for you
doing nothing for me

emancipate yourself
lose the fear and misplaced hope
you brought the shackles
you bound your own feet
emancipate your wounded mind
your opinions you can keep
feet are marching
others are kneeling
you chose your shackles and a back seat
only you can unshackle your feet

8 October 2017
1:22
Bucharest, Romania
KGAT

midnight

it's midnight
in the land of good and evil
most are asleep
dreaming and believing
others walking, pacing
wearing a hole in the floor
the devil in their souls
tweeting and screaming
a sight to behold

it's midnight
the darkness can't hide
the lies and the hate
oozing
swallowing lives
the clock is ticking
counting down the time
when the good will rise
leaving fear behind

it's midnight
in the land of good and evil

a land where skin color is targeted as evil
a land where some make sure the sun won't shine
while others feel the brunt of little minds
darkness is the norm
in this land
it's midnight in the land
brothers and sisters marching
taking a stand

it's midnight
in this land
darkness can't hide
the lies and the hate
oozing
swallowing lives
it's midnight in the land
time will not stand still
the clock is ticking
counting down the time

5 October 2017
21:30
Seattle, WA
KGAT

living numb

i remember the first time
as if it were yesterday
eight months pregnant
a walking watermelon
slowly moving
through the heat of a southern summer
framed by carolina blue skies

on the stale humid air it came:
"look at that nigger"

and there they were
four - blond haired - barely teenaged - males
sitting on the sidewalk
one embarrassed among them said
"hush, she might hear you"
tired and burdened
i kept moving

i
said
nothing

it was the south
it was where i lived
1988
so what if it hurt?

i remember
i was the divorced single mother
of the first grader
who emerged from that belly
a beautiful boy
for whom I swore
life would be different

although knowing the world
i made no promises

i remember
he lost his lunch money
the one dollar bill i gave him
because i was too tired
of making his daily lunch choice
of peanut butter and jelly sandwiches
I was tired of fighting every day to live

she, in his first month
in the first grade
sent a note home
"Patrick had no money for lunch today"
attached to an application

for free lunch
he had no lunch that day

i remember
i showed up to school
the next day
determined to say: I don't qualify for free lunch
i said: "he lost his lunch money yesterday"
she, Ms. White, said: "i thought you needed
assistance"
"So, you let him go hungry?"
what else is there to say?

exhausted before the first bell
i walked away

i
said
nothing
it was the south
it was the school
1994
so what if it hurt?

i am more grown these days
i am wiser
i am older
a few grey hairs
no more teachers to contend with
no more southern life to live

no more little white boys to avoid
in apartment complex parking lots

those little boys are grown men
running businesses
attending meetings
preaching in churches
more unpleasant than they were
in the summer southern sun
in 1988

i remember
a Tuesday morning
me well dressed
ready for travel
ready for another meeting
full of god-talk to end
i smiled as i exited the elevator
i smiled as i entered the lobby
i smiled at the people i knew

and then he said:
"as you were coming this way pushing your
suitcase
I thought you were the housekeeper"
he laughed
at least he called me by my name
that grown white male

i
said
nothing
it was Chicago
it was the church
2017
so what if hurt?

the weariness sets in
with the addition
of one more story
my anger bubbles at boil
every time some white woman
redirects my experience

"I have never seen him act that way before"
"I wonder what he was thinking when he said
that"
"What did you say to make him say that?"
with disregard for my personhood
rendering me invisible
as she buffers for him

again

the tiredness drills slowly into my bones
when the politeness
of hate filled words
and prejudicial rhetoric

fall into the silence
of Jesus filled rooms

my body hurts

every time
the words hit
the dismissive tones land
and i know
there is nothing to say

amidst the institutional amnesia
and selective memory
i remember
the silence of the chosen
i remember
the silence of the ordained
i remember
the silence of the women

I!
REMEMBER!

this is living numb
to ignore the pain directed at
being black
being woman
being different

anesthetized by silence
drugged by indifference
injustice veiled by talk of mercy
sermonizing on loving kindness
consuming tender mercies
while wearing politically correct labels
fiddling with sanctified tabbed collars

so what if it hurts?

it is 2018
the advice comes: "get over it"
the suggestion: "perhaps that is not what he
meant"
the burden: "did you ask her why she said that?"
the response: i claim my numbness
my protection against the blows

there is nothing to say
no story too dreadful
no experience too awful
no encounter too alarming
'cause all can be explained away

so what if it hurts?

16 July 2018
15:24
American Samoa
KGAT

Sierra Leone: tabulay

transformative movements

*We should learn to accept
that change is truly the only thing that's going on
always,
and learn to ride with it and enjoy it.*
—Alice Walker

rivers of Babylon

(Psalm 137)

longing, aching
in the memories of time past
re-living places where my soul
knew home
knew rest
felt belonging.

there was that time
when I knew where I was
knew where to go
knew what was expected
that time, so long ago.

the rivers of certainty are no more
like a life carried by a gentle flow
moving with the current
a part of the undertow
never questioning
being pulled by forces
not my own.

the rivers are no more
nothing feels the same
the boxes destroyed
calm waters are now rough seas
is it wrong to miss the certainty
is it wrong to long for the tame
in the midst of embracing Mystery
in the midst of being re-named?

memories of living amidst expectations
of woman
of Black and Brown skins
of church and being churched
of rooms with no windows and doors
I weep
these days are yet more.

I sit with the Ancestors
by the river and share their tears
longing for HOME
what song shall we sing
in this strange new place
I visit these distant places in my mind
encounter them from time to time

I am no longer their resident
I will sing a new song
of freedom and hope
in this new land
of safe space desired

play it by the book
live cautiously
tread lightly
stay between the lines
nothing to risk
everything to lose
play it safe
follow the rules.

the status quo
guarantees safety
for some but not for all
united we stand
create unrest in the land
where cops throw children
from their seats
of hungry children
of polluted streets
play it safe?
there is no safety
for Black woman or man.

I am a sister
fighting for change
I have no choice
no safety to claim
not safe on the bus
not safe on the street
not safe in my home
not safe in my seat

yet you worry
because I challenge your institutions?

I will push back from the lies you tell
I will suffer rather than live in the hell
you so boldly created for me
you don't get to name me
nor blame me
you don't get to dictate
my race or fate
I choose my religion
I choose to name
my own God
not your will be done.
called for this time
to claim my fluidity
without apology
I am not safe with you
on any level you state
or choose
your very presence
makes this space
unsafe for me.

by the river I sit
with the Ancestors
with the sisters and brothers
with the a'nties, uncs and cousins
longing for a place to call home

longing for where
we can be fully free

31 October 2015
8:20
Lakewood, OH
KGAT

"*mou*"

(*mou* = soft)

the softness of life emerges
on the harshness of grief
hearts filled with losses
finding beds for melodious dreams
swaying like grass growing from cracked concrete

our lives are a contrast of sound
we are silent screens flashing soft scenes
to booming soundtracks
pulsing rhythms gently
overshadowing secrets we keep

mouths moving we practice living
each breath soft
inviting resistance to the hardness of life
willing our participation in excavating self
coaxing surrender to the great unknown

the paleness of dusk brings wings
caught between day and night

we pause in soft light
holding precious each encounter
every moment sacred, tender

holding hearts we travel together
yielding to meaning beyond the coppery glare
ours a journey and witness
to textured shades
soft memories manufactured from unwieldy
expectations

intention produces no accidents
our course takes us where we should be
arriving we welcome change
softly shifting in cocoons of wisdom
we spread timid wings to discover new sensations

16 May 2018
7:33
Seoul, South Korea
KGAT

illusions

I don't wanna see your empty eyes
I don't wanna look
Don't wanna hear your empty cries
Your life like pages ripped from a book

Stalking the world, trying to fill your emptiness
Hiding in the shadows of night
Watching life go by your invisibility
Discouraged by your own wanting
Longing to live whole, to be free

We choose not to see you
Wounds we inflicted, a life we abused
We choose not to see the shackles on your feet
The hurt we caused
A heart broken, an injured soul
We choose not to see
I am you
You are me

I don't wanna see your empty eyes
I don't wanna look

Don't wanna hear your empty cries
Your life like pages ripped from a book

I don't wanna see your empty eyes
From the mirror they stare back at me
I don't wanna look at your bone weary soul
Yet I ache deep inside
Longing to be me, to be whole

I don't wanna hear your cries, your ache
Yet in my sleeping hours, I lie awake
The thunder of your angst overwhelms
The floodgates can't hold back my tears
Broken and afraid you hide
We choose not to see
I am you
You are me

I don't wanna see your empty eyes
I don't wanna look
Don't wanna hear your empty cries
Your life like pages ripped from a book
We want to keep believing
It's easier not to see
I am you
You are me

4 October 2017
5:51
Edmonton, AB
KGAT

rebirth

change comes
sweeping
like the winds of hurricanes
flooding waters rising high
taking with them
doubt
fear

in the midst of change
my heart races
my pulse a staccato beat
my feet cemented
fear a reckoning
not to be forgotten
nothing to hold on to
I sink into the water
I am carried on the winds

I am lifted
carried on the highs
of harsh winds
tumbling into heights

unknown
spiraling into newness
I am reborn.

I am new
there is vision
for this time and space
I rest
renewed
I am in this present
I am in this newness
full of Spirit
I am free

22 February 2017
17:50
Lakewood, OH
KGAT

live you

Live your norm
no fight to live in the shadow of another
live your norm
for this you were born

your freedom is in your chí
the unique energy
you bring to chart your destiny
the road you walk, made for you
a road for one
though others journey with you

Live your norm
no fight to live in the shadow of another
live your norm
for this you were born

I represent me
You represent you
look to the mirror
Ancestors present to lead
to guide you

listen to the beat, the drums you hear
conformity is the message of fear

Live your norm
no fight to live in the shadow of another
live your norm
for this you were born

manifest your destiny Kings and Queens
your light shines brightly
nothing can hide your beauty
no comparisons to be made
you are boldness, courage, brave

Live your norm
no fight to live in the shadow of another
live your norm
for this you were born

this life is yours
Live!
renew your mind
destroy the lies you been fed heavily
lies poison your heart
lies strangle your soul
hear this: your ticket
your ticket for this life
this ticket is made of gold

Live your norm
no fight to live in the shadow of another
live your norm
for this you were born

journey your path
chart your course
live peace and joy
stay your course
avoid those boxes
built to ensnare you
enjoy the journey
embrace what was made for you

Live your norm
Soar high, fly free
Live your norm
separate yourself
no fight to live in the shadow of another
live your norm
for this
you were born

29 August 2017
4:39
St. Catharine's, ON
KGAT

change

this is no light wind
these elements present
no cool breeze kissing the face
providing gentle comfort
these winds of change are strong.

the gentle gust of earlier times
masked the dark clouds
following in their wake
evidence
looming, coming faster these winds
a storm.

the storm of change
with its pregnant clouds
bursting with possibility
for new life
undefined.

the storm holds no fears
the darkness overshadows
that which has to go

all that hides is swept away
and left behind is fertile soil
the sweet smell
of summer rain.

these winds rattle trees
open doors
break windows for newness
to enter
this force of nature
is the Universe at work
demanding that what will be
will be.

these gusts move on by
quickly
they do not linger
their work done
the debris is fodder for the fire
the sky holds no signs
of these winds past
the clear sky
a tapestry
on which birds fly.

11 November 2015
6:27
Lakewood, OH
KGAT

home coming

"*The journey of a thousand miles begins with a single step.*" —Lao Tzu

center yourself at the crossroads of life
believe this moment is where you begin
a future awaits you
your moment is now
the Grandparents bless
the path that awaits
approached from inner knowing

make your way to the river
rest your weary feet
let the waters take you
where your soul longs to be

unshackle your spirit
reconnect to the Unknown
surrender yourself to the unnamed
trust where you are going
light will shine through to guide

follow the path to your destiny
un-afraid, no need to hide

make your way to the river
listen to the waters smoothing stones
these streams refresh
they will renew and make you whole

set aside the burdens you carry
look at your image reflected in the ripples
the sacredness of life coursing by
see your light shining bright
recover your wisdom
reconnect
to those who walk and talk on the other side

make your way to the river
set your mind at ease
open yourself to the Ancestors' whispers
step in the flow and be healed

the fragmented experiences
of brokenness and disconnect
left you wounded
gasping for breath
home bids you welcome to the soul's familiar
there is much to learn
welcome home

make your way to the river
wade in and be washed
in years of tears
despair and hope

make your way to the river
release yourself
to embrace a new vision
receive the homecoming long prepared

19 July 2018
12:08
Toronto, ON
KGAT

walking wounded

"The wound is the place where light enters you"
—Rumi

there is a resident brokenness that sits
quietly humming
yearning for attention
demanding to be seen

these broken places pool with fear
stagnant waters teeming with all that festers
bringing bitterness
lives fragmented, overflowing with despair

we limp along
walking sharp edges
on the borders of fertile grounds that call
yet we resist, afraid

and when we touch the darkness
we feel tiny slivers of light
we hear the music
we feel the emptiness and taste hope

17 July 2018
10:19 PM
LAX - JFK
KGAT

faith journey

hear the voices of the Ancestors
"Come home child, come home"
theirs the call to rituals past
an invitation to learn the Ocean's secrets
unknown

return to the blue skies, they call
come walk our mountains and learn
remember who you are
you are a child of these seas
child come on home

the voices of the Ancestors call again
"Child, listen to each drum beat"
the Universe speaks in mysterious ways
receive of old wisdom to walk these challenging
days

return to the stories of the grandparents
survival, success, impossibilities
remember who you are

find your way home to the deepest knowing, live
life
hear the drum beat

hear the Ancestors speak
"Child, read the prophetic skies"
wisdom carried on the rolling clouds
give yourself to the peace you crave, inside and
out

return to the chants that fill your soul
taste the earth, read the waves
remember who you are
you are a child of the stars, have faith
read the skies

the voices of the Ancestors rise
"Child, touch the wisdom of trees"
thousands of years held in their trunks
fill your fingers and hands with their ancient
healing

return to dreams that kept you awake
smell the revealing sands of time
remember who you are
you were born to speak boldly with souls, reach
out
touch the healing

the voices of the Ancestors cry
"Child, breathe earth's fire"
inhale the memories of generations gone
live into your destiny, for this you were born

return to the spirits who sent you
feel the urgency of now
remember who you are
you were born to swim deep, fly high
breathe the fire

hear the invitation of the Ancestors
"Child, come ride the wind"
believe you are possible
you are the Universe—the earth, water, wind and
fire

return to yourself
grasp the joy that abounds
remember who you are
seeing the unseen
come ride the wind

19 August 2018
12:22
Varadero, Cuba
KGAT

time

There is no way to know
when the time
is right
until it arrives.

There is no announcement,
no invitation to prepare,
no clues to herald
the arrival of loss and change.

Even as it draws closer,
it is elusive,
unwilling to be fixed,
unwilling to be anticipated,
no preparation
can be planned.

We hold on tightly
to that which slips slowly
from our grasp,
with the realization that
life was never ours

to hold or own,
with the knowledge
that breath is a gift.

The time comes
and then it is gone,
taking with it breath,
leaving wonder,
nightmares,
awe and chills.

The memories linger,
haunting.
The images present
themselves as mirages
in a wilderness
of grief and loss.

Over time,
a distant future
promises peace
where there is none.

We wait for time
to ease the ache,
unwilling
to feast on tears.

17 July 2018
23:10
LAX-JFK
KGAT

inheritance

ours is no solitary journey
we are invited to travel
accompanied by generations
calling us into our deeper selves
whispering to us of our wisdom and strength

we are travelers
ours a journey back to the self
we dispel the projected myths excavating truth
we return to knowing why we came
receiving validated memories others labelled as
misguided fantasies

we dream of tomorrow, of clarified embedded
understandings
we plan yesterday holding to unrevealed mysteries
walking beyond time we traverse today boldly
inheritors of keys to unspoken visions
we live defying history, rewriting our stories

we are intentional in moving
water making streams

dirt making mountains
we are more than we appear to be
we find our way to redefining greatness

we awaken from imposed inferiority
escaping the bindings of mental enslavement
we hear before we understand
we see before we know
guided by our surrender we navigate to greater
than we

we ease anew into the flow
willing that we live whole
we emancipate the aspirations of generations
yesterday, today, tomorrow
walking together hearing the same drums beating
in our veins

19 May 2018
6:54
Seoul, South Korea
KGAT

Nigeria: udu

Epilogue

the drums

i will not explain
why i don't comb my hair
why my clothes don't look like yours

listen to the beat
tell me if you hear
the beating of the drums

you say you don't understand
what i do
how i think

you say you don't know
what i wear

you say you don't understand
what i say
how i feel

listen for the beat
tell me when you hear
the beating of the drums

I will not explain
why i shave my head
why i live my live as i do

the music drives my life
the music you won't hear
the beating of the drums

listen for the music
tell me when you hear
the beating of the drums

the music drives my life
the music you can't hear
the beating of my drums

24 March 2004
11:33
Kissimmee, FL
KGAT

Drums In Our Veins

Lightning Source UK Ltd.
Milton Keynes UK
UKHW020721090223
416597UK00011B/576